Wandering Woolly

by Andrea Gabriel

Little Woolly poked her head out from between her mama's warm, furry legs. She wondered about the world beyond.

A toad croaked. Woolly followed the hopper, trying to touch it with her trunk. The voices of her aunties rumbled in her ears and vibrated in the ground. *Everything is safe*, the sounds told her.

The sun was very hot on her back. Woolly saw the river flashing silver and cool, and wanted to splash the water over her head.

"Let's go!" she called to her mama. But the other mammoths were busy picking grasses with their long, two-fingered trunks. All they ever wanted to do was eat grass. She would go by herself!

The river roared as ice and boulders tumbled downstream in the spring thaw. Little Woolly did not hear her mother trumpeting to come back. It wasn't safe!

Crash! Ice splintered and toppled off the glacier. Woolly was thrown into the rumbling, rolling water.

The little mammoth fought to keep her trunk above the water, trumpeting and trumpeting for her mama. *Whoosh!* The river raced past a ground sloth grazing in the trees.

A log bobbed in the waves. The little mammoth caught up to it and rested her legs across the top. She was very tired!

The water sped past a hunting lion, but Woolly was safe in the center of the current.

She floated past a short-faced bear, a giant beaver, and humans camped near the river. She could smell the smoke of their fires and hear the barking of their hunting dogs.

At last the river grew wide, and the current slowed. Little Woolly was exhausted, but she scrambled onto dry land, desperate to get back home. She put her head low to the ground, touching it with her trunk.

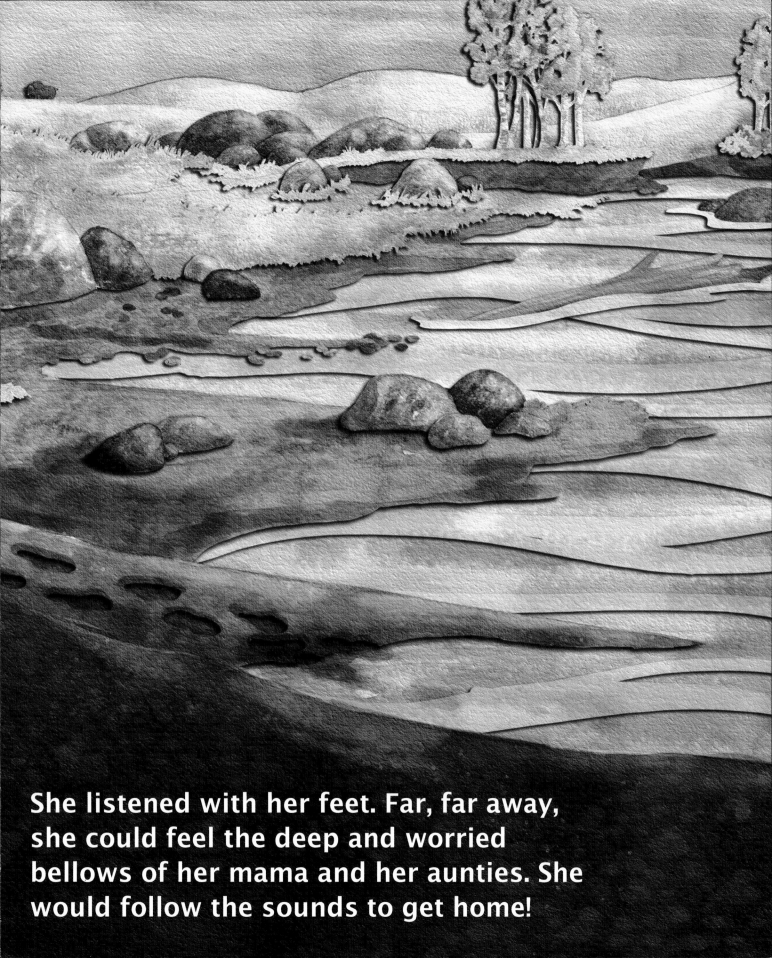

She listened with her feet. Far, far away, she could feel the deep and worried bellows of her mama and her aunties. She would follow the sounds to get home!

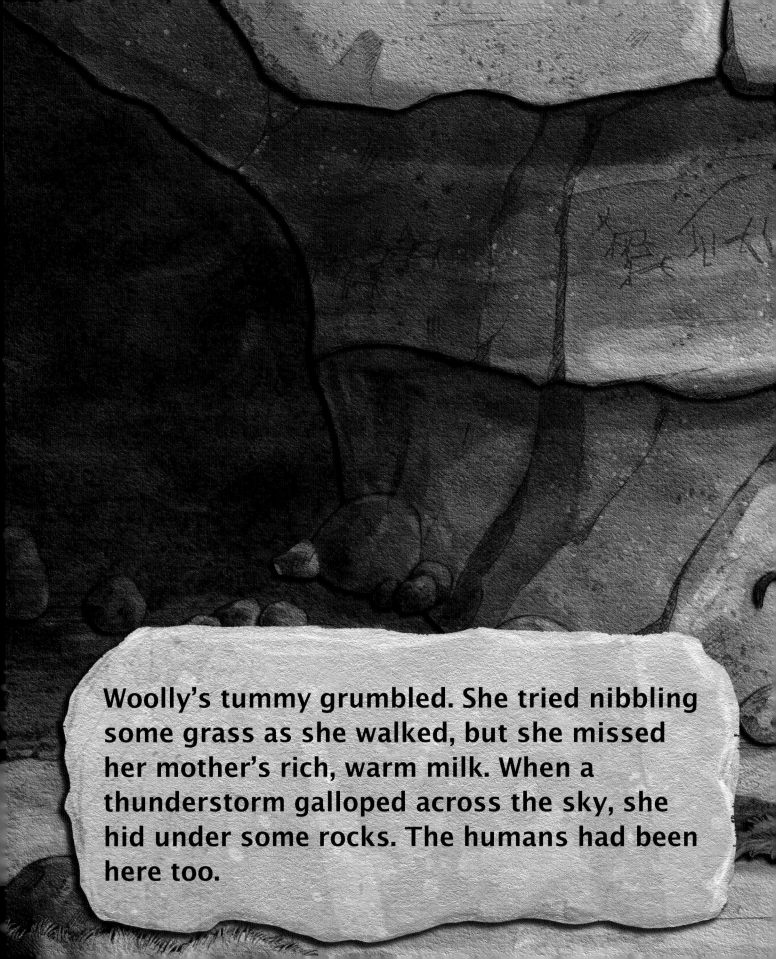

Woolly's tummy grumbled. She tried nibbling some grass as she walked, but she missed her mother's rich, warm milk. When a thunderstorm galloped across the sky, she hid under some rocks. The humans had been here too.

The storm passed, and the sun returned. Little Woolly smelled a family of saber toothed cats napping in the grass. She wandered far away from them, following the rumblings of her herd. She could feel their voices in her feet. Mama and her aunties were very worried!

At last, she could see them! The brown backs of her family rose above the grass. Woolly ran forward, trumpeting her return. The other mammoths rushed to greet her. They touched her with their trunks and bellowed with happiness to have their Woolly back home again.

Little Woolly tucked her head into her mama's warm, furry legs. She was glad to be home!

For Creative Minds

Ice Age Sequencing

An ice age is a time when the world's climate is very cold and much of the earth is covered in ice. This ice builds up into large sheets, called glaciers. Glaciers can be thousands of feet deep. Over time, they expand across the land or shrink to a smaller area. Use the dates to put these images in order (from oldest to newest) to spell out the word and find out what happens to a glacier at the end of an ice age.

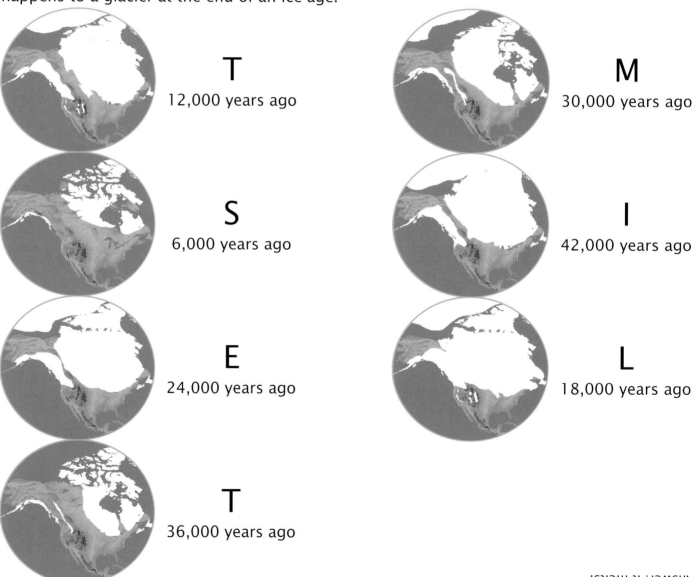

T
12,000 years ago

M
30,000 years ago

S
6,000 years ago

I
42,000 years ago

E
24,000 years ago

L
18,000 years ago

T
36,000 years ago

Answer: It melts.

Mammoths and Elephants

The last woolly mammoths died 4,000 years ago. When a type of animal doesn't exist any longer, scientists say that animal is extinct. Even though mammoths are extinct, they still have living relatives—elephants. Read about mammoths and elephants below. How are they alike? How are they different?

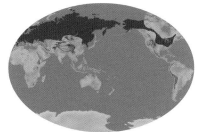
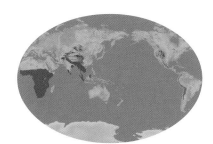

Mammoths lived in North America, Europe, and Asia. There are two different kinds of elephants: African and Asian.

Woolly mammoths had shaggy fur all over their body. This fur kept them warm their whole lives. Elephants have bristly hair. As elephants grow, they lose their hair.

Woolly mammoths were 9-13 feet (2.75-4m) tall. African elephants are 10-13 feet (3-4m) tall. Asian elephants are 6.5-11 feet (2-3.5m) tall.

Mammoth herds were made of related females and their young. The oldest female mammoth led the herd. Elephant herds are made of related females and their young. The oldest female elephant leads the herd.

Woolly mammoths had long, curved tusks. Large males had tusks 15 feet (4.5m) long. African elephants and male Asian elephants have tusks up to 10 feet (3m) long. Female Asian elephants have short tusks or no tusks at all.

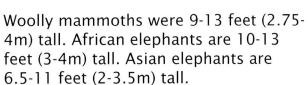

Scientists can learn about mammoths by observing elephants. Elephants have wide, flat feet. Their feet feel vibrations in the earth caused by sound from miles away. Mammoths had wide, flat feet. Do you think it is possible that mammoths could hear with their feet, like elephants do today?

The Clovis people were some of the first humans in North America. We know about the Clovis people because of scientists who study ancient people. These scientists are called archeologists. They study bones and objects made by people who lived long ago. They can tell us what tools the Clovis people used, what they ate, and how they lived.

The Clovis people lived 13,500 to 11,000 years ago. They made spearheads, called Clovis points. When archeologists find these spearheads, they know Clovis people lived in that area. The map below shows where the Clovis people lived.

Some Clovis people hunted and ate Columbian mammoths. Archeologists have found mammoth bones near Clovis villages. They have even found some mammoth fossils that were injured by Clovis points.

Some Clovis people lived in small towns. Hunting parties, like the one in this story, moved from place to place to follow their prey—like a mammoth herd. They lived in round, wooden huts.

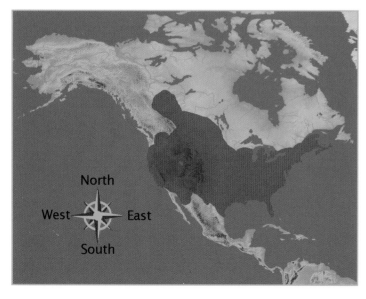

Clovis points were 1.5-8 inches (4-20 cm) long and 1-2 inches (2.5-5 cm) wide.

Extinct Ice Age Animals

American lions were one of the largest cats to ever live. They weighed 560-775 pounds (256-351kg). These fierce hunters had long legs and powerful muscles. American lions went extinct 11,000 years ago.

Giant beavers were over 8 feet (2.5m) long. They weighed up to 220 pounds (100kg). Like beavers today, the giant beavers gnawed on trees. Giant beavers went extinct 10,000 years ago.

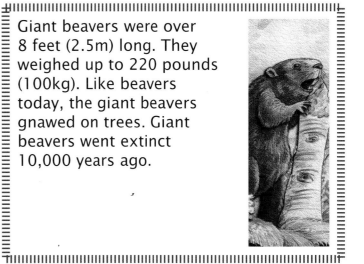

Modern sloths live in trees, but giant ground sloths spent most of their time on the ground. They lived in both North and South America. Ground sloths ate only plants (herbivores). Giant ground sloths went extinct 13,000 years ago.

Two different kinds of saber-toothed cats lived in North America. Smilodon cats had saber-teeth 7 inches (18cm) long. Scimitar cats' teeth were 4 inches (10cm) long. Saber-toothed cats went extinct 11,500 years ago.

The short-faced bear was the largest meat-eating animal (carnivore) in North America. When they stood on their back legs, they were 8-12 feet (2.4-3.6m) tall. They could run at 40 miles (64 km) per hour. Short-faced bears went extinct 11,000 years ago.

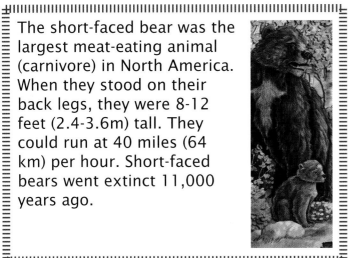

Mammoths were plant-eating animals. Adult mammoths needed to eat 400 pounds (180kg) of food each day! Their tusks grew through their whole life. Scientists can tell how old a mammoth was when it died by the number of rings in the tusks. Mammoths went extinct 4,000 years ago.

For my parents. Thank you for sharing your love of wildlife, science, and geologic time.—AG

Thanks to Deb Novak, Director of Education, and Gary Morgan, Assistant Curator of Paleontology, at the New Mexico Museum of Natural History & Science, for reviewing the accuracy of the information in this book.

Library of Congress Cataloging-in-Publication Data

Gabriel, Andrea, author, illustrator.
  Wandering Woolly / by Andrea Gabriel.
      pages cm
  Summary: A young woolly mammoth chases a toad to the river and tumbles in when the glacial ice breaks, then must make a difficult journey, sneaking past cave lions, bears, and humans, trying to return to her herd. Includes an activity and facts about the Clovis people and Ice Age animals.
  ISBN 978-1-62855-558-5 (English hardcover) -- ISBN 978-1-62855-567-7 (English pbk.) -- ISBN 978-1-62855-585-1 (English downloadable ebook) -- ISBN 978-1-62855-603-2 (English interactive dual-language ebook) -- ISBN 978-1-62855-576-9 (Spanish pbk.) -- ISBN 978-1-62855-594-3 (Spanish downloadable ebook) -- ISBN 978-1-62855-612-4 (Spanish interactive dual-language ebook) 1. Woolly mammoth--Juvenile fiction. [1. Woolly mammoth--Fiction. 2. Animals--Habits and behavior--Fiction. 3. Glacial epoch--Fiction.] I. Title.
  PZ10.3.G114Wan 2015
  [E]--dc23
                                              2014037326
Translated into Spanish: *Lina Lanuda, la vagabunda*
Lexile® Level: 660L
key phrases for educators: climate, early humans, extinct, history, mammoth,

Bibliography:
Elephants "Hear" Warnings With Their Feet, Study Confirms. (n.d.). Web. Retrieved November 20, 2014, from
    <http://news.nationalgeographic.com/news/2006/02/0216_060216_elephant_sound.html>.
Haynes, C. V., Stanford, D. J., Jodry, M., Dickenson, J., Montgomery, J. L., Shelley, P. H., Rovner, I. and
    Agogino, G. A. (1999), A Clovis well at the type site 11,500 B.C.: The oldest prehistoric well in America.
    Geoarchaeology, 14: 455–470.
Lange, I. (2002). Ice Age mammals of North America: A guide to the big, the hairy, and the bizarre. Missoula,
    Mont.: Mountain Press Pub. Print.
Lister, A., & Bahn, P. (2007). Mammoths: Giants of the Ice Age (Rev. ed.). Berkeley, Calif.: University of
    California Press. Print.
Mammoths of the ice age [Motion picture]. (1995). WGBH.
Mueller, T. (2009, May). Ice Baby: Secrets of a Frozen Mammoth. National Geographic Magazine. Print.
Raising the mammoth [Motion picture]. (2000). Discovery Channel Video.

Thanks to the following photographers for releasing their elephant photos into the public domain (in order of appearance): Andrew McMillan, International Affairs Library (USFWS), and Nuzrath Nuzree.

Clovis point based on an exhibit viewable at the Natural History Museum of Utah, Salt Lake City, Utah.

Manufactured in China, January, 2015
This product conforms to CPSIA 2008
First Printing

Arbordale Publishing
Mt. Pleasant, SC 29464
www.ArbordalePublishing.com